HOLLY AND THE SKYBOARD

Holly wishes she had a skateboard, but her parents can't afford to buy her one. But on her seventh birthday, Holly gets the present of her dreams!

Although a relative newcomer to children's books, Ian Whybrow has already earned considerable acclaim as a comic writer, with his popular series of stories about Sniff the dog. His first picture book story, *Quacky Quack-quack!* (illustrated by Russell Ayto, published by Walker Books), was shortlisted for the 1991 Smarties Book Prize. He is also the author of *The Time Sailors*.

Tony Kenyon has illustrated numerous books for young readers, including *Jam for Tea*, *Gordon in the Garden* and several educational titles.

D1045617

Some other titles

Beware Olga!
by Gillian Cross

Pappy Mashy
by Kathy Henderson

Jolly Roger
by Colin McNaughton

IAN WHYBROW

HOLLY and the SKYBOARD

Illustrations by Tony Kenyon

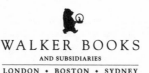

WALKER BOOKS
AND SUBSIDIARIES

LONDON • BOSTON • SYDNEY

For my darling niece, Holly Jones Warren,
who dreamed it all up
I. W.

First published 1993 by
Walker Books Ltd, 87 Vauxhall Walk
London SE11 5HJ

This edition published 1994

2 4 6 8 10 9 7 5 3

Text © 1993 Ian Whybrow
Illustrations © 1993 Tony Kenyon

Printed in England by Clays Ltd, St Ives plc

British Library Cataloguing in Publication Data
A catalogue record for this book is
available from the British Library.

ISBN 0-7445-3182-9

Contents

Chapter One

On the morning of Holly's seventh birthday, Holly got up and did her chores as usual, even though it was her special day.

When she felt she'd done a good job, she opened her present from her mum and dad. It was a hand-knitted pullover with a skateboard pattern on the front.

Holly said it would look good with her red hair.

"Sorry we couldn't afford a real skateboard," sighed Dad. He knew how much Holly had wanted one.

Her mum said, "There's a lovely surprise for you today. Guess what! Your cousin Richard is coming over to play with you! Won't that be nice?"

Holly didn't like telling lies, but her mum looked so pleased, she couldn't hurt her feelings. "Just what I wanted on my birthday!" she said bravely.

Richard arrived in a big car driven by his nanny. He was a big rude boy with a big bottom. He was carrying the most *unbelievably* expensive skateboard in the whole world, all covered in fabulous stickers.

He also had a very small package
which he gave to Holly.

"Here you are, Carrot Head," he said. "It's a book of stamps. Don't forget to stick one on your thank you letter, will you? Good joke, eh?" And he laughed, blah ha ha!

I wish he wouldn't call me Carrot Head, thought Holly.

Chapter Two

Five minutes after Richard arrived, he said, "This is so *boring*! What are we supposed to do all day when you haven't even got a telly in this dump?"

"Why don't we go skateboarding?"
Holly suggested. Every night, ever
since she could remember, Holly
had dreamed about skateboards.

In the dream she had a skateboard
with magic buttons on it. If she
wanted to do a fantastic trick, all
she had to do was press a button.

She looked longingly at Richard's skateboard, hoping that perhaps he would let her try it out.

"No way!" Richard snapped. "I bet you haven't even got a skatepark here or anything."

Holly said no, they didn't have a skatepark, but there was a quiet bit of roadway out the back. "Why don't we go and see?" she said.

There was a good slope that went down and down, then up in front of some big blue garage doors.

"There are some super bumpy parts here," said Holly. "They would be fun for lying down. And there's a drain to dodge by the kerb."

"What do you know about it, *girly?*" said Richard. "And what does that stupid old man want?"

Holly turned to see her next door neighbour, Mr Windrush, waving to her over his back gate. "Happy Birthday, Holly," he called. "Would you and your cousin like to come into the workshop and see the present I've made for you?"

"*I'm* not coming!" shouted
Richard. "I hate home-made
presents!" And with that, he jumped
on his fancy skateboard and
whizzed off down the slope.

Chapter Three

Holly ran over to the gate. "Don't take any notice of him, Mr Windrush," she said. "He's just a bit spoilt. He can't help being rude."

"Well," said the old man, "I hope you won't be disappointed. My work looks very rough and plain."

When Holly saw the skateboard lying on Mr Windrush's workbench, she wasn't just surprised; she was *astonished*. She jumped, just as if somebody had popped out from behind the sofa and shouted Hey!

Because the skateboard was *exactly* like the one she had been riding in her dreams, right down to the round buttons on the top! All she could say was, "Gosh, Mr Windrush! I don't *believe* it! Thank you, thank you, thank you!"

It made Mr Windrush very happy to see how pleased Holly was. He shut the gate after her, gave it a contented little pat and went indoors.

Richard was busy showing off, so he didn't notice that where the tips of Mr Windrush's fingers had tapped the gate, two little branches had sprung up and sprouted rainbow-coloured leaves and clusters of chocolate fudge bars.

Chapter Four

"What a piece of *junk*!" laughed
Richard, when he saw Holly's new
skateboard.

Holly took no notice. She lay on her skateboard and enjoyed the lovely curvy feeling she got as it picked up speed down the slope.

"Too peasy!" shouted Richard. "Watch me and I'll show you what you can do on a *real* skateboard!"

He turned his hat round and
showed Holly how he did
Standies, Kneelies,
Wheelies and Jumpies.
He went really fast
and he never fell
off, not once.

Then he showed
her the big lump of
plastic at the back, so
you could stamp down
and make the board jump up.
"Bet you haven't got *this*," he said.

"I haven't got any plastic, but I have got these special buttons," said Holly. She got off her board and pointed to the four round steel buttons set into the wood.

Richard laughed and said they were just screwheads. "They hold the wheels to the board, Carrot Cake!" he scoffed. "*Anybody's* got those. They're not special. Look!"

He pressed down hard on one of his and showed her the white cross-shaped dent the screwhead made in his fingertip.

Holly had been thinking. Her birthday skateboard looked exactly the same as her dream skateboard – but perhaps it wouldn't *do* the same things in real life. Still, she held her breath, thought of her very favourite drink – and firmly pressed the top button on the left.

Chapter Five

Suddenly Holly was sipping
something delicious through a pink
bendy straw – a cold Coca-Cola
with a bubble gum ice-cream float
and a cherry on top.

"Would *you* like one of these?" she asked.

Richard was so surprised, he fell flat on his big bottom. "Gimme one!" he shouted.

"Please," said Holly.

Richard had to say the word, even though he hated it.

"Please," he begged.

Holly pressed the button again
and quick as a flash, Richard had
a paper cup full of the most
wonderful drink he had ever tasted –
cold and fizzy, with a
really big scoop of
the best bubble
gum ice-cream
ever. *Ever!*

Would you like one of these?

He couldn't
believe his
eyes. "Where
did this come
from?" he
demanded.

"I just pressed one of the special buttons, that's all," explained Holly. She sucked hard and made the Coke rattle in the bottom of her cup. "Ahhhh!" she gasped as she finished. "Just what I needed."

She put the empty paper cup
down on her skateboard, and as
soon as it touched the dull brown
wood, the cup went $\{?\}\{?\}\{?\}\{?\}\{?\}$
and vanished.

Richard's mouth dropped open in
amazement.

"Let's go skateboarding!" laughed
Holly.

Chapter Six

For a minute, when Holly seemed
to be doing magic tricks, Richard
was lost for words. But as soon as
he heard her say, "Let's go
skateboarding!" he found his
voice again.

"Watch me!" he yelled, dropping his cup. "Because this is going to be *hard*, Miss Special Buttons!"

He raced down the slope, screaming his head off, jigged to avoid a pothole, bent his knees and neatly bounced the skateboard up over a kerb, before spinning it round and stopping it in a flurry of dust in front of the garages.

"Try *that* on your stupid piece of wood," he panted.

Holly lay face down, her legs sticking out like a frog's.

That made Richard laugh. She
took no notice, but pointed herself
down the slope, right at Richard,
and kicked off with her toes.

With her nose just above the
road, she was soon going even
faster than Richard had done.

As
Holly
rushed
nearer, her
red hair flying out
behind her, Richard
started to get nervous.

If she didn't do something soon –
drag her baseball boots along the
ground or roll off sideways – she
would crash into the kerb, or
be smashed to pieces
against one of
the garage
doors!

Chapter Seven

Richard put his arm over his head
and made himself as small as he
could, expecting to be bowled over
like a skittle.

That was when Holly pressed a
button and her skateboard lifted its
nose and took off like a plane.

It rose smoothly over the roofs of
the garages, and then soared higher
to skim the tops of some trees.

Holly looked down at the
cottages below, shrunk to the size
of toys. Richard looked no bigger
than an earwig. Holly pulled up the
nose of the skateboard and looped
the loop. Then she leaned,
swooping down to snatch a black
and white feather from an empty

magpie's nest, and stuck it in her
hair. Pink smoke came out of the
back of the skateboard and she
wrote her name in joined-up letters
in the sky. Then she dived and
landed expertly on the road before
rolling down to where Richard was
still glued to the spot.

"Let's go in and have some lunch now, shall we?" Holly said, cool as a Coca-Cola with a bubble gum ice-cream float.

Chapter Eight

All through lunch Richard sat looking
at the magpie feather in Holly's hair
and wondering how he could get
the magic skateboard off her.

Finally, he had a very cunning idea.
When the car came for him,
Richard ran up to Holly's mum and
gave her a big kiss (which he had

never done before) and said, "Thank you very much for having me," (which he had never done before) and then he said, "Before I go, I would like to give Holly my fabulous, expensive skateboard and I'll just have her ugly old home-made one. How about that?"

Holly was too surprised to answer, and as for her mum and dad, they thanked Richard for coming, thinking what a lucky girl Holly was to have such a generous cousin.

Chapter Nine

Holly wandered out into the garden
with Richard's skateboard and
sighed a sad sigh.

"What's the matter, Holly?" came
a voice from the other side of the
fence. "Has your cousin left you?"

"I hope you won't be upset, Mr
Windrush," sniffed Holly, "but
Richard's taken the lovely
skateboard you made for me and
left me his."

"I'm not at all upset, Holly," said Mr Windrush. "As a matter of fact, I'd say you made a jolly good swap. May I have a closer look?"

Holly passed it over the fence. Mr Windrush held it just with the tips of his fingers, touching the beautifully smooth wood and feeling the cool metal strip along its edge. "Why, this is a *dream* of a skateboard," he smiled, as he handed it back.

When she took it in her arms once more, Holly was surprised to notice that it had four round steel buttons where the screwheads had been!

"Happy skyboarding, Holly!" said Mr Windrush.

Chapter Ten

Meanwhile, out on the motorway, there was a big traffic jam.

And in the middle of the big traffic jam there was a big car.

And in the back seat of the big
car there was a big rude boy with
a big bottom.

And the big boy with the big
bottom let out a big scream.

Because no matter how hard he pressed the buttons on his home-made skateboard, all he got was a little white cross-shaped dent on the tip of his finger!

MORE WALKER PAPERBACKS
For You to Enjoy

☐ 0-7445-3103-9   *Art, You're Magic!*
by Sam McBratney /
Tony Blundell   £2.99

☐ 0-7445-3188-8   *Beware Olga!*
by Gillian Cross / Arthur Robins   £2.99

☐ 0-7445-3173-X   *Jolly Roger*
by Colin McNaughton   £2.99

☐ 0-7445-3189-6   *Little Luis and the Bad Bandit*
by Ann Jungman / Russell Ayto   £2.99

☐ 0-7445-3095-4   *Millie Morgan, Pirate*
by Margaret Ryan /
Caroline Church   £2.99

☐ 0-7445-3096-2   *Pappy Mashy*
by Kathy Henderson /
Chris Fisher   £2.99

☐ 0-7445-3092-X   *The Snow Maze*
by Jan Mark / Jan Ormerod   £2.99

☐ 0-7445-3094-6   *Tillie McGillie's
Fantastical Chair*
by Vivian French / Sue Heap   £2.99

☐ 0-7445-3102-0   *The Unknown Planet*
by Jean Ure / Chris Winn   £2.99

**Walker Paperbacks are available from most booksellers,
or by post from B.B.C.S., P.O. Box 941, Hull, North Humberside HU1 3YQ**

24 hour telephone credit card line 01482 224626

To order, send: Title, author, ISBN number and price for each book ordered, your full name and address,
cheque or postal order payable to BBCS for the total amount and allow the following for postage and
packing: UK and BFPO: £1.00 for the first book, and 50p for each additional book to a maximum of £3.50.
Overseas and Eire: £2.00 for the first book, £1.00 for the second and 50p for each additional book.

Prices and availability are subject to change without notice.

Name _____

Address _____

_____